ASHLEY WOLFF

Stella & Roy

Dutton Children's Books
NEW YORK

FOR MY DEAR ROWAN

Library of Congress Cataloging-in-Publication Data
Wolff, Ashley.   Stella & Roy / by Ashley Wolff. — 1st ed.   p. cm.
Summary: Even though Stella's bike is much faster than Roy's,
he manages to win their race around the park because she
keeps stopping to enjoy its natural beauty.
ISBN 0-525-45081-5   [1. Parks—Fiction. 2. Bicycles and
bicycling—Fiction. 3. Racing—Fiction. 4. Nature—Fiction.]
I. Title.   PZ7.W821234St   1993
[E]—dc20 92-27005 CIP AC
Published in the United States 1993
by Dutton Children's Books,
a division of Penguin Books USA Inc.
375 Hudson Street, New York, New York 10014
Typography by Adrian Leichter
Printed in Hong Kong
First edition
1   3   5   7   9   10   8   6   4   2

This book is illustrated with linoleum block
prints hand-tinted with watercolor.

One Sunday in spring, Stella and Roy took their bikes to the park. Stella's had three blue wheels and was built for speed. Roy's had four wheels, a wooden seat, and streamers dangling from the handlebars. It was built for coasting.

"Hey, Roy," called Stella. "I'll race you around the lake.
Last one to the popcorn stand is a rotten egg!"

Stella pedaled away as fast as she could,

but around the first curve she spotted a tree good for climbing.

"Roy is such a slowpoke," she said to herself. "He'll never catch me." So Stella stopped and counted eleven turtles, three sea gulls, and a frog.

And Roy rolled right on by.

When Stella finished counting, she leapt back on her bike and pedaled past Roy. "See you later, alligator!" she called as she whizzed by.

But in the pool below the waterfall, a flash of orange caught her eye. So Stella stopped to let the fish nibble her fingers.

And Roy rolled right on by.

When the fish swam away, Stella jumped back on her bike and pedaled off. "In a while, crocodile!" she called as she raced past Roy.

But in the meadow near the swings, Stella stopped again. While the geese crowded round, she picked a big bouquet of buttercups and dandelions.

And Roy rolled right on by.

Stella hopped back on her bike and sped away once more. "Bye-bye, housefly!" she called to Roy as she passed him. But in the shade of the old pine, she met Officer Rowan and her horse, Mister B. So Stella stopped again.

And this time Roy rolled all the way to the popcorn stand.

Stella finally said good-bye to her two friends and pedaled away as fast as she could. As she rounded the final curve, there was Roy, waving.

"Rotten egg!" he yelled. "Rotten egg!"

"May I have some popcorn?" asked Stella politely. "Please?"

"On the moon, baboon!" said Roy.

But he was a good sport. He let her take a big handful all the same.